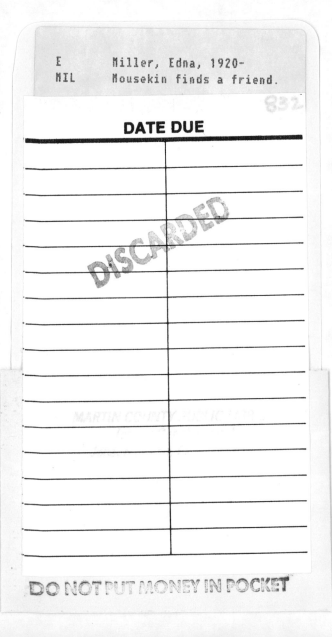

MOUSEKIN FINDS A FRIEND

MOUSEKIN
FINDS A FRIEND

Simon and Schuster Books for Young Readers
Published by Simon & Schuster Inc.
New York

To My Mother

Simon and Schuster Books for Young Readers
Simon & Schuster Building
Rockefeller Center
1230 Avenue of the Americas
New York, New York 10020
Copyright © 1967 by Edna Miller
All rights reserved
including the right of reproduction
in whole or in part in any form.
Published by the Simon & Schuster Juvenile Division
SIMON AND SCHUSTER BOOKS FOR YOUNG READERS is a
trademark of Simon & Schuster Inc.
Manufactured in the United States of America
10 9 8 7 6 5 4 3 2

10 9 8 7 6 5 4 3 2 (pbk)
Library of Congress Catalog Card Number: 67-18924
ISBN 0-13-604224-4
ISBN 0-671-66973-7 pbk

The day song had ended.
All the voices
that fill a forest by day
had said, "Good night."
Mousekin felt lonely
as he waited for the peeper's call
and for the night song to begin.

Only when the mist
had hidden every leaf
and sheltered every nest
did the peeper call from its hiding place, "Phw-eep."
Far off another answered, "Sl-eep!"

Then, as if by magic,
the night was filled with sound.
Clicks and whistles,
hoots and howls,
echoed back and forth in the forest.
Mousekin sang one note—
as sweet as any bird...
but no one answered *his* call.

Mousekin was about to sing
another mouse-song
when he saw a figure,
much like his own,
scurry along the branch above him.

He raced up the branch
to meet his new mouse friend
but *it* hurried away down another.
They hopped to the right
and darted to the left
until the two of them came suddenly
face to face.

There are many things
that can fool a mouse
in the forest.
There are moths that look like owls
and birds that look like mice
and a misty night in springtime
can make them all seem real.

The furry little bird
scolded Mousekin
for being such a fool...
for not knowing a real mouse
from a titmouse
and for giving her such a fright.

Mousekin rap-a-tapped his paw so fast
that he made the catkins jump
along the branch beneath his feet.
He had never been tricked like this before!
He knew a cattail couldn't bite
nor a pussy willow chase him.
A catfish never caught a mouse—
though a real live cat just might!

Mousekin stopped his angry tapping
when he heard a rustle
in the leaves close by.
Then he saw a shadow.
Was it a mouse's ear?

With a squeak of delight
Mousekin chased after the little form
as it disappeared into the leaves
on the forest floor.
He searched all around the foxglove
that grew beneath the tree.
There was no mouse to be found.

Only a fox-finch
ruffled its feathers
and peered into the night
to see what moved below.

Mousekin was so eager to find a friend
he almost forgot that
a real live fox might be mouse-hunting too.

When he came to the foot
of the dogwood tree
(where the dogtooth violets grow),
he heard a friendly sound.
Mousekin leaped and found
the nibbling and munching he had heard
was not a mouse at all...

...but a box-turtle
shell-deep in wild strawberries,
eating his fill.

Mousekin reached for a berry
and nibbled it thoughtfully.
The old turtle, wise in his turtle-years,
looked at Mousekin for a long while
before he swallowed and said,
"I've seen lots of mouse-ear by the stream."

Mousekin raced to the edge of the water
that skipped and splashed
as it curved its way into the forest.

There he saw hundreds of pretty blue flowers
growing all about,
with leaves as soft and as dainty
as a mouse's ear...
but there was no other mouse to be seen.

Mousekin remembered
that forget-me-not and mouse-ear
were just different names
for the same little flower.
Above him, in the darkness,
he heard a turtle dove coo, "Fool...fool."

Mousekin washed his face,
brushed his ears,
cleaned his whiskers...
and pretended not to hear.

Another figure sat nearby
and cleaned its whiskers too.
It washed its face,
brushed its ears,
then tapped its foot much faster
than any fairy drum.

Mousekin spun around
and just caught sight
of a mouse's tail
as it disappeared into a hollow log.

Once again, he chased after the shadowy form.

When Mousekin reached the other end,
he stopped and peered around.
The little shape with the wiggling tail
had vanished again.
Could the mousetail growing near the log
have played him such a trick?

More lonely than before,
Mousekin wandered in and about
the long grasses.
He never even heard the bull frog's
warning call, "Mouse-hound! Mouse-hound!"

The weasel sprang from its hiding place
beside the mossy hollow,
but stopped in surprise to see...

...not one but *two* white-footed mice
leap for the nearest tree.

They raced to the topmost branches
and jumped into an empty nest...
pulling fluff and feathers all around them
and 'way up over their heads.

In the warmth of the nest,
Mousekin found a creature
just like himself.
A squeak that answered his squeak...
a chirp that answered his chirp...
The day song would soon begin
and Mousekin's search was over.